The Tooth Fairy Trap

To Riley -
Dream big,
Brush well!!
Rachelle Burk

by Rachelle Burk

illustrations by Amy Cullings Moreno

For Cara and Alana,

and the tooth fairies who danced on their pillows.

The Tooth Fairy Trap

WiggleRoom Books
11 Brookhill Road, East Brunswick, NJ 08816

ISBN: 978-0692228814

Printed in the USA

Contents

Cara
Bradley
Erin
Alex
Lisanne

THE LIST

Bluma knelt under the toadstool and laid out her supplies: A sack of fairy dust, her silk tooth bag, and a few coins.

Faylene, an Elder Fairy, flew down from a hollow in the willow tree. "Do you have everything you need?" she asked.

"All ready!" said Bluma.

"Well then, here's your list for tonight."

Bluma took the scroll from the wise old fairy. Her face brightened as she read some of the names. Suddenly she let out a gasp. "Bradley again!"

"The last visit could have been a disaster," Faylene said. "Don't let your guard down this time."

"I'll be careful," promised Bluma.

"Use plenty of fairy dust," Faylene warned, "but for goodness sake, hold your breath when you sprinkle it." She shook her head and sighed. "A tooth fairy allergic to fairy dust! Whoever heard of such a thing?" She smoothed Bluma's wings. "And remember, my dear, tooth collecting is not a time for play. Make your rounds quickly and stay out of trouble. You know what could happen."

Bluma blushed. She did not want to go back to polishing teeth with the younger fairies. "Yes, Faylene." She curtsied low. Her daisy-petal dress fanned out against the myrtle vines that covered the garden bed.

"One more time now, my dear—let's hear the safety pledge."

Bluma cleared her throat and recited:

"When I prance upon a bed,
I'll use my dust, my wings, my head."

The worried look disappeared from Faylene's eyes. "Off you go then. Be back before the last blink of the firefly."

Bluma gathered her things and fluttered from the garden.

DEAR
Fairy
THE TOOTH
IS IN THE
BOX LOVE
BRAD

FAIRY TRAP!

Bluma flew to Bradley's room first, eager to put the task behind her. Once inside, she huddled against the windowpane. She took a deep breath and looked around the room.

In the corner, a canary slept in a cage with its head beneath its wing. An iguana snoozed in a tank on the dresser. Goldfish circled in a bowl on a shelf cluttered with plastic dinosaurs.

I bet he'd like to add me to his collection, thought Bluma.

The last time she was here, Bradley had lined glass marbles along the windowsill. They glistened like colored stars in the bright moonlight. *What beautiful stones,* Bluma had thought. The blue one shimmered like a rushing stream. Bluma touched it, causing it to roll into the others. One by one, the marbles dropped to the wooden floor. Clack, clack, clack! Before she knew it, Bradley awoke and nearly managed to snatch her with a swoop of his butterfly net.

"He won't trick me tonight," Bluma said to herself. "I'll use my dust, my wings, my head."

Bradley twitched in his sleep. A bit of drool pooled on the side of his lips. Bluma tossed a double dose of fairy dust over his bed, holding her nose so she wouldn't sneeze.

She inspected the room and discovered a note taped to thc lamp.

Dear Fairy,
The tooth is in the box.
Love, Brad

A shocbox sat beneath the bedside lamp with its lid propped open with a stick. Bluma perched on the rim of the box and peered inside. In the dim light, she could see Bradley's tooth tied to a string at the bottom of the stick.

"Another fairy trap!"

"Good luck figuring that one out," squeaked a voice. Across the room, a hamster watched Bluma through the bars of his cage. "You're

going to end up in here like me," he said. "Spinning your wheels, but getting nowhere." He jumped on the exercise wheel and began to run.

Bluma tugged nervously at her dress. A daisy petal fell loose. "He's a tricky boy, but it's my job to get his tooth and leave a coin. Any ideas?"

The rodent hopped off the wheel and chewed on a wooden toy. "Maybe you can pry open his mouth and yank out a different tooth." He flashed his long teeth. Bits of sawdust stuck to his furry chin.

Bluma shook her head. "I'm sure the Elder Fairies have rules against that." She examined the trap.

"Perhaps I can untie the knot around the tooth." As she flew down into the cardboard box, the flutter of her wings caused the stick to quiver. The lid of the box shook above her.

She quickly returned to the top. Her heart pounded wildly in her chest.

"Can't say I didn't warn you," said the hamster. He spit out a splinter. "Last week the kid tried to trap a lizard."

Bluma's eyes grew wide. "What happened?"

"It got away, but the poor green fellow had to leave its tail behind."

Bluma shuddered and pulled again at her dress. Another petal dropped off. "This will take a little thought," she said, wiping the sweat from her brow. "I'll come back later." She flew from the house, leaving Bradley's tooth behind.

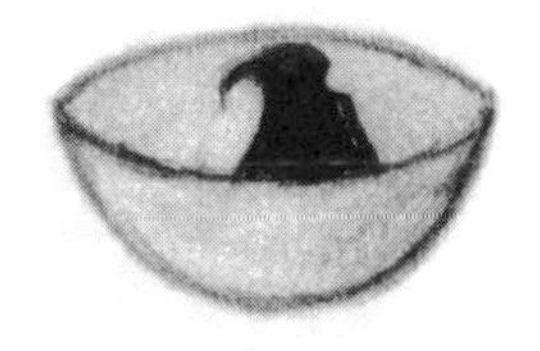

TREASURE HUNT

Wonderful things awaited Bluma in Erin's room. She fluttered about like a bee in a clover patch, touching the delights around her. There were games, coloring books, and cut-out paper dolls. There were wooden animals, finger paints, and a glass jar brimming with sweets.

She picked up a piece from a jigsaw puzzle on the floor and set it in place. "This one goes here!" As she picked up another, she remembered Faylene's words: *Tooth collecting is not a time for play.*

"I'd best get started on finding that tooth." She sprinkled a handful of fairy dust over the bed. All at once, her eyes watered and she felt a tickle in her nose.

"Ahh…ahh…"

Her hand flew to her face and she pinched her nose until the feeling went away. "Pesky allergy," she mumbled as she glanced around the cluttered room. Then a tingle of excitement rose in her belly. "I wonder where Erin has hidden the tooth tonight!"

Erin loved to play games. The first time she lost a tooth, she laid a path of peanuts to lead Bluma to its hiding place. The next time, Bluma had to unroll a ball of yarn to reach the tooth tucked inside. She left behind a fuzzy string trail that ran through the bedroom, across the hall, and into the kitchen. The last tooth was the most fun of all. Erin had dropped it to the bottom of the goldfish bowl, and Bluma had to dive for it as if it were a sunken treasure!

Ready for tonight's adventure, Bluma wiggled under the pillow and emerged with a gold ring. She clapped with delight. "This clue is easy." She flew to the dresser and heaved open the lid of a velvet jewelry box.

"Well, this doesn't belong here," she said, untangling a bookmark from the web of necklaces and bracelets. "It must be clue number two."

Bluma eyed the titles of the books stacked onto the bookshelf: *Tree House in a Storm*...*A Good Sign for Alice*...*Don't Turn the Page*....

In the middle of the shelf sat a book with bold letters: *Tooth Fairy Trap*. A black shoelace dangled from between its pages. Another clue. Bluma tugged the lace until it slipped free.

She studied the shoes scattered about the closet and shook her head. "There's nothing unusual in here." Then she spied a pair of soccer cleats sticking out from beneath the bed. Only one of them had a shoelace.

"Aha! It matches the one Erin left in the book." Bluma started to

weave the lace onto the shoe, until she had an idea.

"Maybe I could use this to help me climb into Bradley's trap. I'm sure Erin won't mind if I borrow it for the night." She stuffed the lace into her tooth bag and hopped inside the shoe.

"What's this?" Hidden near the toes, she found a miniature teacup and saucer. "Of course!" Her pulse raced as she scrambled from the shoe and flew to the dollhouse.

A tiny doll family sat around the dining room table, set with fine china on a lacy tablecloth. "Good evening," Bluma greeted politely as she took the empty chair. "Is it time for tea?"

She lifted the lid off a silver teapot. Erin's pearly tooth sparkled inside.

"Ta-da!" Bluma held up the tooth like a trophy. "We'll celebrate with dessert."

She peeked inside a covered dish. "A chocolate chip—my favorite! Would everyone like a piece?" As she served the boy doll a slice, the sly grin painted on his face reminded her of Bradley. Her tummy flipped.

"I bet *you* could tell me how to deal with a tricky boy like Bradley."

The doll stared blankly across the table.

Bluma shrugged and licked the chocolate from her fingers. She bid goodbye to her hosts, returned briefly to Erin's bed, and flitted away to the next house.

A shiny coin lay nestled under the pillow. And on Erin's cheek was a smudge of chocolate, left by a fairy's kiss.

JUST KIDDING

Bluma squeezed under Lisanne's pillow and felt around. She dragged out a small matchbox decorated with glitter and sparkly beads.

"What a pretty tooth box," she said, turning it over to examine the artwork. She slid it open and removed the tooth, replacing it with a silver coin.

"That was quick. I might get home on time for once. Faylene will be pleased." She dropped the tooth into her bag. On the way out, a scribbled sign tacked to the wall caught her eye.

Tooth Farey,
This way to Blaine's tooth→

An arrow pointed to the other bed.

"Blaine? How can that be?" Bluma scratched her head and unrolled her scroll. "There is no Blaine on my list." She fluttered across the room and hovered over Lisanne's little brother.

The child looked like an angel, breathing softly under the thick quilt.

Bluma shrugged. She held her nose, sprinkled a bit of glittery dust, and squeezed under Blaine's pillow. A moment later, she dragged out a small box covered with cartoon stickers and bits of colored yarn.

Inside the box, Bluma found a soft, lumpy tooth. Something wasn't right. She rolled it around in her hands. She sniffed it. The tooth was made of clay!

"Trying to be like your big sister, are you?" She smiled at the boy and slipped the clay tooth into her bag.

"I wouldn't want to disappoint you, then."

She reached into her bag for a coin, but quickly withdrew her hand. The Elder Fairies had strict rules against leaving real money for fake teeth. The lesson was clear.

"Don't be fooled, make no mistake!
Leave no money for a fake."

"It seems to muddle the magic," Faylene had explained. "Then, when those children lose real teeth, their names don't show up on our list."

Bluma bit her lip as she watched Blaine suck his thumb. "I suppose Faylene knows best, but the poor boy will surely cry if he finds nothing under his pillow." She tugged at her dress. "What to do, what to do…?" Petals drifted down to the bed sheets.

Then a smile spread across her face. She held up a silver coin and sprinkled it with a pinch of fairy dust. Pop!

"Perfect!" She tucked the gift under the pillow and flew off to the next house.

In the morning, Blaine could show off his prize—a soft, lumpy coin, made of clay.

TRY, TRY AGAIN

Bluma again peered into Bradley's bedroom window. "Time to try again. Be brave, be brave," she said to herself.

A lizard scampered across the brick wall. He had a swollen stump where his tail should be.

"Excuse me," Bluma called. "Do you know the boy Bradley?"

The lizard stopped and turned to her. "I know one thing—I wouldn't go in there if I were you."

"I'm afraid I have to. And I could use a bit of help if you wouldn't mind."

"Sorry, can't get involved," said the lizard. He darted away and disappeared around the house.

Bluma took a deep breath and slipped quietly into Bradley's room.

She peered into the fairy trap. "If I can somehow attach the shoelace to the box, I can slide down into the trap without disturbing the stick." She searched the room, but could find nothing to fasten the lace.

"Psst. Hey, Fairy." The hamster hung on the bars of his cage. "Got anything to eat in that bag?"

Ah, here's someone who can help me! Bluma thought.

She flew to his cage. Chewed bits of wooden toys and cardboard scraps littered the pine shavings that covered the cage floor.

"Doesn't Bradley feed you?"

"Mostly his mother does. I'd starve to death if she left it up to that kid. All he gives me is a crumb now and then, when he steals cookies from the kitchen."

"Gee, I'm sorry to hear that."

After an awkward silence, Bluma cleared her throat. "Yes, well…I wonder if you would consider helping me get that tooth?"

The hamster pretended not to hear her. "I don't even *like* cookies. What I really crave is a crunchy walnut. Or maybe a nice turnip." His eyes narrowed. "Do you like turnips, Fairy?"

Bluma understood. He might help if she offered him something in return. "Well, yes, but I don't usually carry them with me. Maybe next time I come—"

"What's in the bag, then?" he interrupted.

Bluma glanced down at her tooth bag. "Just coins. And the teeth I've collected so far tonight."

"What about that one?" He nodded towards her other pouch. "You wouldn't mind sharing a bit of your lunch, would you?"

Bluma lifted the sack of fairy dust. "Oh, this isn't my lunch. It's dust."

The hamster rolled his eyes. "Dust. Yeah, sure it is." He crawled to the corner of the cage, curled up, and closed his eyes.

"No, really! Let me show you." She yanked the sack open so quickly

that a cloud of fairy dust poofed into the air.

"Ahh…CHOO!" Bluma tumbled backwards. "Excuse me!" she said. She scrambled to her feet and wiped off her dress. "It's hard to believe, but I'm allergic to this stuff."

The hamster didn't answer. He was sound asleep, his fur glistening with fairy dust.

PEN PAL

I'll come back later for one more try, Bluma thought, as she again left Bradley's house without the tooth. *I do hope the hamster won't sleep too long.*

Next on her list was Cara's house. Inside the bedroom, Bluma wound up the ballerina music box. She danced on Cara's nose to the familiar tune:

It's a small world after all,
It's a small world after all…

Tap, tap, twirl. Tap, tap twirl. "Gosh, all this music and dancing better not wake you!" Bluma shouted over the music, tapping and twirling as hard as she could.

Cara didn't stir.

"Oh, I almost forgot the dust," Bluma yelled. She tossed fairy dust into the air. "Ahh-Choo! Oops, forgot to hold my breath again!" She looked hopefully at Cara, but the child slept soundly.

Bluma's shoulders slumped. "Hmph! I wish you would wake up so we can play together. Of course, the Elder Fairies have rules against that anyway, don't they? So many silly rules!"

She poked around beneath the pillow, humming along with the music box. As usual, Cara left a letter with the tooth. Bluma skipped across the page and read the words printed neatly in purple ink.

Dear Bluma,
How have you been? Did you win that butterfly race? You'll never believe what happened today! My doll, Katie, fell off the chair during our tea party, and her tooth broke off. Now we're both missing a tooth! Poor Katie—I'll grow a new one, but she won't.

Bluma gazed up at the doll on the shelf. Katie stared back with a gap-toothed smile.

Bluma grinned and opened her tooth bag. She flew to the shelf and molded a piece of Lisanne's clay tooth into Katie's mouth.

"Katie, you have a beautiful smile!" she whispered, standing back to admire her work. Satisfied, she flitted to the desk and lifted Cara's pen. It towered over her as she dragged it across the paper.

Dear Cara,
I would have won the butterfly race, but I had a problem. Just before the big day, I broke my wing swinging on an ivy vine. My wing has healed, though now I have a bigger problem.
Remember I wrote to you about Bradley? Well, he has set another trap...

The ballerina twirled slower and slower on the music box until the melody stopped. Bluma finished the letter and slid it under the pillow with her shiniest coin. She stroked her

friend's soft curls. "How long will it be till I can visit you again?"

Just then, Cara stretched her mouth in a wide yawn. Bluma reached in and quickly felt a few teeth. One of them wobbled!

She smiled. "It won't be too long."

PET PEEVE

Bluma perched on the edge of Alex's bed and listened in the darkness. The boy mumbled something about dump trucks and ice cream, flopped over beneath the blanket, and fell silent again.

"Sheba? Are you in here?" Bluma peered through the shadows.

"Shhh! You'll wake the puppies!" whispered Sheba.

"I was so excited for Alex's tooth to fall out so I could see your pups," said Bluma, fluttering down from the bed. "How many?"

"Five." Sheba beamed. "Four boys and a girl."

Bluma laid her tooth bag on the rug. "This is for you," she said, handing Sheba a teeny bone tied with a ribbon of spider silk. With a sprinkle of dust, it sprang to full size.

"How sweet of you!" said Sheba. She licked Bluma's face and chomped on the juicy bone.

Bluma smiled and wiped her cheek. "My pleasure." She watched Sheba gnaw and nibble, her strong teeth whittling away at the bone. *Those teeth can chew through anything,* thought Bluma. *Just like Bradley's hamster.*

The hamster's teeth! Could that be the answer to Bradley's trap? As Bluma thought of a plan, she moved toward the pups who were snuggling against Sheba's warm body. She reached out to pet one.

Sheba dropped the bone. "Ross is a light sleeper, so you'd best not…," she started to warn, but it was too late.

Ross popped up, wagged his tail, and snatched Bluma's tooth bag.

"Oh no!" Bluma cried, and tried to grab it back, but the puppy dove under the bed. He stuck out his head with the bag dangling from his mouth.

Sheba looked sternly at Ross. "Put it down, dear."

Bluma tugged at her bag, but he refused to let go. His eyes begged her to play with him.

"Pups will be pups," Sheba sighed, shaking her head. "Alex can't even get them to 'sit' or 'stay' yet."

"May I use a bit of fairy dust?" asked Bluma.

"Of course."

Bluma tossed a pinch from her pouch. In a firefly's flash, Ross yawned. The tooth bag fell from his

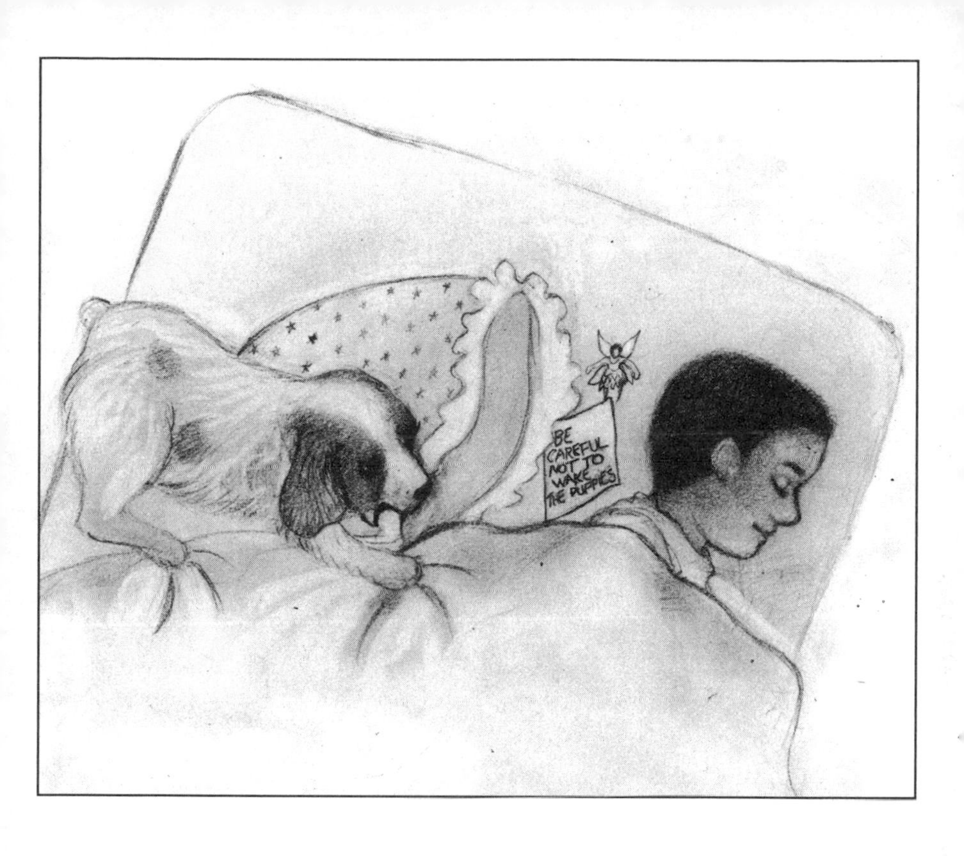

mouth. Bluma lifted the soggy bag with her fingertips. It dripped with puppy slobber. "Good dog," she whispered, though he had already fallen asleep.

"Your pups are lovely," Bluma said.

"Thank you. I'm so glad you could visit." Sheba then turned her attention back to the bone.

"Well, I'd better get back to work." Bluma flew to the bed.

"Let me help!" Sheba jumped onto Alex's bed and tugged the pillow from under his head.

Bluma found the tooth folded carefully inside a note.

"What does it say?" asked Sheba.

"It says, 'Be careful not to wake the puppies.'"

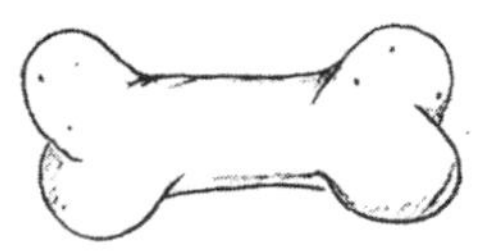

THE GAME PLAN

Outside Alex's house, Bluma checked her bag to be certain Ross had not lost anything. Four teeth, a few coins, and a wad of clay left over from Lisanne's fake tooth—everything seemed to be in place.

She rubbed her sleepy eyes and gazed at the faint light that glowed on the horizon. A firefly flew circles around her. *Blink, blink, blink!*

"Yes, I know it's late," Bluma replied, "but I have one more tooth to collect."

She dashed back to Bradley's house. His room was quiet, except for the sound of the hamster scampering in his cage. He turned his back to the fairy.

Bluma flew over to him. “Mr. Hamster,” she said, bowing her head, “I’m sorry about the dust. It was an accident.”

The hamster ignored her. She moved closer and poked her nose through the bars. “I’m in quite a fix, and could really use your help with this fairy trap.”

“Sorry,” said the hamster without looking up. “I’m fresh out of good ideas.” He gnawed what was left of the wooden toy. Bluma watched his razor teeth grind the wood into tiny flakes.

"You've already given me a great idea," she said, "but I can't do it alone. If I let you out, would you help me get the tooth?"

He stopped nibbling and squinted at Bluma. "A taste of freedom is tempting. What else can you offer?"

"I'll throw in a tasty treat."

He shook sawdust from his whiskers and grinned. "You got a deal! And hey, call me Scraggs."

Bluma giggled.

"Yeah, I know," grumbled Scraggs, glancing over at Bradley. "How *do* they come up with these names?"

Bluma unlocked the cage and the door swung open. "The problem is that the flutter of my wings will knock over the stick and close the lid," she explained. "So I need you to crawl inside the trap and chew the tooth off the string. Then I'll toss in a coin."

"Why don't you stick the money under the pillow? Isn't that how it's usually done?" asked Scraggs.

"Usually, yes. But look."

Strips of sticky flypaper surrounded Bradley's pillow like a moat.

"Ah, more traps," Scraggs chuckled. "Clever boy."

"The sun is rising, so we don't have much time." She watched anxiously from the rim of the box as Scraggs crept over the side and into the bottom of the trap. “Careful! Don’t jiggle the stick!” she said, tugging at her dress. A wilting petal dropped to the table.

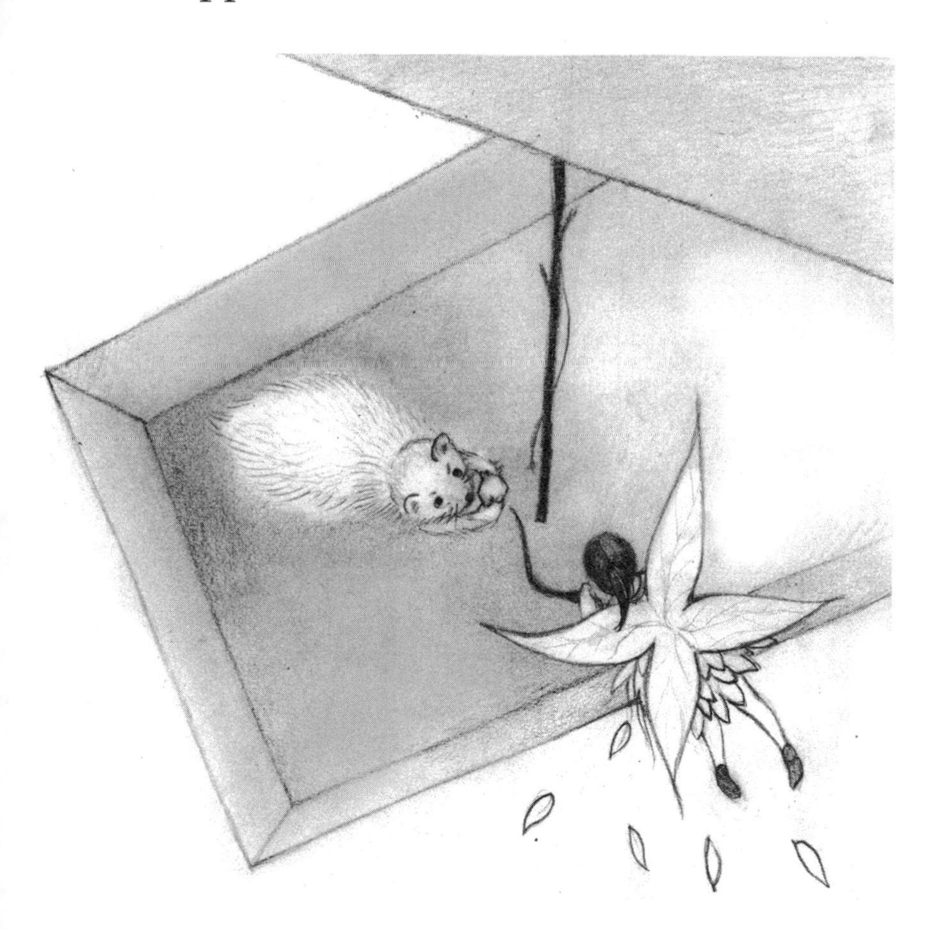

"I know what I'm doing," Scraggs snapped. He gnawed at the string tied to the tooth.

A dim light streamed into the window. "Can't you go a little faster?"

Scraggs shot her an angry look but continued to chomp. Finally, the tooth broke free.

"Quickly, now! Bring it up!"

The rodent sneered. "You don't really expect me to carry that disgusting thing up in my mouth, do you? The kid doesn't brush so well, you know."

Bluma groaned. She thought for a minute, and then opened her tooth bag.

"Attach the tooth to this." She stuck a wad of Lisanne's clay tooth to the end of Erin's shoelace and lowered it into the trap.

Scraggs pressed the tooth into the clay with his paws. "Ready!"

Bluma pulled it up. "Well done!" she cheered.

"Yeah, whatever," said Scraggs. "Just throw him a quarter and let's get out of here."

Bluma tossed a coin into the trap. It bounced on the bottom, went into a spin, and landed against the stick. Before Scraggs could scramble from the box, the lid smacked shut.

"Couldn't you wait till I got out?" he snarled. His voice was muffled inside the trap.

"Scraggs!" Bluma called. She struggled to lift the lid. It wouldn't budge.

"Forget it, Fairy," he called to Bluma. "I can get myself out. But remember—you owe me. A deal's a deal."

She heard him scratch and munch inside the wobbling box. *I did make a promise,* she thought. She pulled out a coin and sprinkled it with fairy dust. "Something good to chew."

Pop! Poof! A crunchy turnip coin rested in the palm of her hand. She tossed it into the cage and gathered

her things.

Suddenly Bradley stirred. He blinked his eyes. The fairy dust Bluma sprinkled hours earlier had worn off, and now the scraping and scurrying inside the box had woken him. Bradley sat up and sprang towards the trap. “Gotcha, Fairy!” he shouted, clutching the box.

But Bluma had already escaped into the dawn.

GOOD NIGHT

A pink sun peeked over the horizon. The last stars flickered and disappeared.

Bluma yawned as she slid the tooth bag off her shoulder and tucked it under the toadstool. She brushed her teeth with a sprig of mint and washed her face with a drop of morning dew.

"How was your night?" asked Faylene as Bluma curled up on her bed of soft moss.

"Five teeth! Only one fake this time."

"And Bradley?" Faylene eyed the few remaining petals of Bluma's tattered dress.

"No need to worry. He's no match for me."

"So…you used your dust, your wings, your head?"

"Yes, and a little help from a furry friend."

Faylene's eyes widened. "You didn't get friendly with a stray cat again, did you? I thought you learned your lesson!"

"No, no. Nothing like that," said Bluma. "He was a darling, barely bigger than a field mouse."

"Ah." Faylene relaxed. "A good night's work, then." She covered Bluma with a rose petal and kissed her forehead. "Sleep well, my dear. I hear there are seven children with loose teeth. Tomorrow could be a busy night."

Bluma snuggled under the velvety petal and closed her eyes.

"Yes, a good night's work," she murmured. "A very good night."

With the last blink of the firefly, she drifted off to sleep.

The End…

(Until the next lost tooth)

Actual letters between the author's daughters and their tooth fairies.

Hi! My name is Cara. When I am in bed at nite can you try to wake me up so I can see you? I promis I will not hurt you.

Deer Cara I danst on yur nose and you didint wake up ha ha. wares yur tooth?

Dear tooth Fairy
What is your Name
How old Are you
do you like my tooth
Box? ps write BACK
do you no my nam!
Love Alana

Deer Alana
Thank you for riting to me. Most kidz just wunt muny. I am Lioli. Yur sistr noze me. I like her. You luk like her when you sleep. I luv yur box. It sparklz like Faery Dust. Dont ferget to brush cuz I like nise teeth! LUV,
Lioli

dear Lioli When is your birthday? How do you cech food if you live in this tree And What do you eat? love

Dear Alana
I dont no wen my birthday is cuz fairies dont do that. I eet seedz and berrys and hunny. The beez share. Wen I get striky I wash in a puddl. It's fun. Love Lioli

Dear Steena,
I am getting to know you very well. Do you have a mother and father? Can you draw a picture of yourself for me? How do you know when a child looses a tooth? Have fun!
Love,
Cara

Deer Cara,
I have a mother and a father.
I just no when sumwun loozez a tooth.
I don't no how to draw. I'l try.
Love
Steena

Dear Tooth Fairy,
What is your name?
What do you do with the teeth? If a child is awake do you still go in the childs room? Do you ever get scared of people? Can tooth fairies be boys and girls? Tonight, can you wait for me to wake up in the morning? I really want to see you. If you can't, can we be pen pals?
Cara

Deer Cara,
Moira sez yoo cant see me, not allowd. Boy faeries mak seedz gro. Thare not for teeth. I can onli come if thare is a tooth so if yoo want me to come back I will haf to leev yur tooth and that meenz no monee OK? My name is Steena, yoor last one wus Lioli. Babeez get yoor teeth but the Grow Faeries give them. Im not scard of peeple cuz they nevr see me thare alwayz sleeping and grow nups dont see cuz thay dont beleev. Wen yoo dont beleev we wont come and then yoor mom haz to.
Lov, Tooth Faery Steena

Dear Steena or Lioli,
I have a few questions... Do you wash the teeth before you give them to babys? Is it hard to squeeze through window cracks? Where do you get all of the money from?
I lost this tooth yesterday at camp. Do fairies have camp?
Love,
Cara

Dear Cara, Lioli iz bizzy playing with litening bugs so I am geting yur tooth. We cleen teeth by rubing them with sand. They shine! Its eezy to skweez throo windows but sumtims we hafe to tri a fyu. We find muny that peepl looz and save it to pay for teeth. Fairys dont hav camp but we get to wach kidz play thar and sleep in tents. When we laf kidz think its bugs!
Love Steena

Rachelle always wanted to be a tooth fairy.

ABOUT THE AUTHOR

Rachelle Burk is a writer of fiction, nonfiction and poetry for children.

Her work has appeared in national publications such as *Highlights for Children* and *Scholastic Science World* classroom magazines.

Rachelle is a popular children's entertainer, performing as "Mother Goof Storyteller" and "Tickles the Clown." In a parallel life, she works as a social worker and rescue squad volunteer.

The New Jersey author loves to share the joy of reading and writing through dynamic **School Author Visit** programs. For more information, visit her website:

www.rachelleburk.com

Other books by Rachelle Burk

Tree House in a Storm

Don't Turn the Page!

Sleep Soundly at Beaver's Inn

Miss Crump's Funny Bone
(chapter book)

The Walking Fish
(middle grade novel)